Survive

Chris Buckton
AR B.L.: 3.0
Points: 0.5   MG

SURVIVE

by Chris Buckton
illustrated by Paul Savage

Librarian Reviewer
Marci Peschke
Librarian, Dallas Independent School District
MA Education Reading Specialist, Stephen F. Austin State University
Learning Resources Endorsement, Texas Women's University

Reading Consultant
Mary Evenson
Middle School Teacher, Edina Public Schools, MN
MA in Education, University of Minnesota

STONE ARCH BOOKS
Minneapolis San Diego

First published in the United States in 2008
by Stone Arch Books
151 Good Counsel Drive, P.O. Box 669
Mankato, Minnesota 56002
www.stonearchbooks.com

Originally published in Great Britain in 2006
by Badger Publishing Ltd.

Original work copyright © 2006 Badger Publishing Ltd
Text copyright © 2006 Chris Buckton

Library of Congress Cataloging-in-Publication Data
Buckton, Chris.
    [Survival]
    Survive / by Chris Buckton; illustrated by Paul Savage.
    p. cm. (Keystone Books)
    Originally published: Great Britain: Badger Publishing Ltd., 2006,
under the title Survival.
    Summary: When brothers Mark and Pete get separated while hiking
up a mountain, one of them almost does not make it back to the family
campsite.
    ISBN-13: 978-1-59889-852-1 (library binding)
    ISBN-10: 1-59889-852-3 (library binding)
    ISBN-13: 978-1-59889-904-7 (paperback)
    ISBN-10: 1-59889-904-X (paperback)
    [1. Hiking—Fiction. 2. Brothers—Fiction. 3. Survival—Fiction.]
I. Savage, Paul, 1971– ill. II. Title.
PZ7.B882339Sur 2008
[Fic]—dc22   2007003020

1 2 3 4 5 6 12 11 10 09 08 07

Printed in the United States of America

Table of Contents

Chapter 1

Stay Together

"Whatever you do, remember to stay together," Dad said.

It was the first time Mark and Pete had gone climbing on their own.

They were camping with their parents.

They'd spotted a mountain that looked easy to climb.

They begged their parents to let them try it.

"You know we're good climbers," said Mark. "We know all of the safety rules."

"We'll stay on the trail," promised Pete. "It's a really nice day. Nothing will go wrong."

"The weather forecast said there would be fog later in the afternoon," warned Dad.

"We'll be back by then," Pete said.

Their parents looked at each other.

Mom nodded. "I think we can trust them," she said. "We can drive into town while they're climbing."

"Have you thought about what to take with you?" asked Dad.

"Yes. We made a list," said Mark.

STUFF TO TAKE:
MAP
WATER BOTTLE
ROPE
PHONES
FLASHLIGHT
FIRST AID TIN
SANDWICHES
CHOCOLATE
MATCHES
COMPASS

"Good," said Dad. "I'm glad to see you thinking for yourselves. Who's going to get everything ready?"

"We are!" the boys said.

The boys worked fast. They wanted to get going on their climb. They checked their climbing shoes, tying the laces tightly and folding down their thick socks.

Finally, they were ready. They each carried a backpack.

Dad said, "Whatever you do . . ."

"We know, stay together!" replied the boys, laughing.

Chapter 2

HIGHER AND HIGHER

The climb was easy at first. It was good weather for climbing. It wasn't too hot, and the cool breeze gave them energy.

"I could climb forever on a day like this!" shouted Mark.

"I could make it up Everest!" yelled Pete.

They followed the grassy path along the side of the mountain.

The path was rocky farther ahead. They could see a waterfall sparkling in the sun.

"Let's get to the rocks and then stop for lunch," said Mark, panting. The trail was getting steeper.

They found a flat rock to sit on while they ate their lunch. They looked down into the valley far below.

"Look, you can see the campsite," Mark said.

"The cars look so small! They look like you could pick them up and play with them, like toys!" Pete said.

"There's the road that goes to town," Mark said, pointing.

There was nobody else in sight on the mountain. The only sound was the rushing water as it fell over the rocks.

"This is the life!" said Pete, as he lay back in the sun. "Just wait until we tell the guys back at school."

"We're not at the top yet," warned Mark.

"We will be soon." Pete jumped up. "Come on, let's get going!"

Chapter 3

THE SKULL

The boys climbed slowly. They had to scramble over rocks. They couldn't see the top of the mountain.

"Our water bottle's empty," said Mark as he took the last drink. "Let's fill it from the waterfall. The water's really clean up here."

The waterfall was a little off the trail, but they would be able to get back easily.

"Stay on the path!" joked Mark in his dad's voice. They laughed as they left the trail and climbed across to the waterfall. Pete went first. Mark followed his brother.

Suddenly they heard a low moaning. It sounded like a trapped animal. "What was that?" asked Mark.

"I don't know," said Pete, moving toward the sound.

Pete suddenly stopped. He saw something on the ground. It shined white in the sun.

"Hey, look! It's a ram's skull!" he shouted.

"Well, that noise didn't come from a ram's skull," called Mark. "It came from a real, live animal."

"There are no real, live animals anywhere up here," Pete replied, picking up the skull.

The brothers had walked a long way from the trail. The waterfall was very steep.

"It's getting too dangerous," shouted Mark. "Let's forget about the water and get back to the trail."

Mark looked down. He felt a chill of fear and suddenly lost his footing.

The water bottle fell out of his hands and bounced from rock to rock. It disappeared into the valley below.

"Mark! We need that!" shouted Pete.

"I didn't do it on purpose," Mark replied, getting his balance back.

They slowly made their way back to the trail.

Pete was holding the ram's skull.

"Get rid of that thing," said Mark. "It gives me the creeps."

Pete found a triangle of rocks and put the skull on top of them.

Just then, two climbers came around the corner of the trail. They were heading down the mountain.

One of them called out. "Hello there. Are you coming or going?"

"We're on our way up," Pete replied with a smile.

"You should turn back," said the climber. "There's fog at the top. And it can get thick very quickly."

TURNING AROUND

Mark watched the other climbers until they were out of sight.

Suddenly he felt scared.

"Pete!" he said. "You heard what they said. We should start back."

Pete wouldn't listen. "It's not far. We can't give up now," he said.

Pete started climbing again.

"Pete, come back!" shouted Mark.

"You're a wimp!" said Pete with a laugh.

"I'm not coming with you," shouted Mark.

"Think I care?" Pete said, quickly walking forward.

"We promised to stay together!" Mark yelled.

"Well, you'll just have to come, then," Pete told him. "I'm not turning around now. We're too close."

"How can you be so stupid?" Mark said angrily. "We could get lost in the fog! Climbing in fog is dangerous! We told Dad we'd be careful."

Pete just kept climbing up the mountain. "Scaredy cat!" he yelled.

Mark looked up toward the mountain top. He could see fog swirling around the highest peak.

"I'm going back down. And so will you if you have any brains at all," he told his brother.

Pete stopped and looked back at Mark. He shrugged. "See you later, then," he shouted at Mark.

Mark turned his back on his brother and started going back down the mountain.

Chapter 5

THE WAY DOWN

Mark walked slowly.

He was sure that Pete would follow him soon.

Every now and then, he stopped and turned around, hoping to see his brother coming quickly down the trail behind him.

He could still see the skull on the rocks where Pete had left it.

It seemed to be smiling at him.

He tried yelling one more time. "Pete!" he shouted.

His voice echoed around the rocks. No one answered.

"Whatever. See if I care!" he shouted.

Why should he worry? He'd done the right thing.

Maybe Pete was teasing him.

I bet that Pete is following me, Mark thought.

His brother must be tricking him. He would follow Mark and then scare him by jumping out at him.

Mark stopped and listened.

He could hear the waterfall. Nothing else.

It was really hard to climb down the mountain.

The rocks were slippery.

Sometimes, Mark couldn't see the trail clearly and he had to stop.

It would be even more difficult in the fog.

What if Pete couldn't find the path? What if he fell into the waterfall?

Mark still felt angry at his brother.

"It's not my fault," he said to himself. "I tried to make him come back with me. I hope he gets really scared. It would serve him right."

There was a sign by the edge of the trail.

Mark hadn't seen it on the way up.

Mark's heart beat faster. Maybe he should go after Pete and warn him.

Then he remembered that he had his cell phone. Great! He could call Pete.

He tried to call his brother, but there was no answer.

Chapter 6

KING OF THE WORLD

At the top of the mountain, the fog surrounded Pete. It was getting colder, and the fog felt wet on his face.

Drops hung on his cap and got into his eyes. It was so quiet inside the fog that every sound was muffled. He couldn't even hear the waterfall.

Standing on the top made it all worthwhile. Pete felt like the king of the world.

A ray of sunlight broke through the fog for a moment.

Pete could see right down into the valley below.

He thought about Mark. He must be back at the campsite by now.

Pete thought that it was stupid of Mark to give up and miss the great view from the top of the mountain.

Then the fog folded back like a huge blanket, and Pete was inside it. He couldn't see anything. He knew he had to get down, but he wasn't sure which way he'd come up.

He remembered that Mark had the map, but the compass could help. Pete got it out of his backpack and figured out which way was north.

He had to think really hard to find the direction of the campsite. He thought he remembered seeing the sun set in the west behind the mountain. So he needed to go east.

He walked for a while, and there was the trail! He was right. Pete felt proud of himself. He'd be back in no time. Mark wouldn't have much to say when Pete told his story at school!

Chapter 7

PETE'S NOT BACK

When Mark reached the campsite his parents weren't back from their shopping trip.

He took his shoes off and lay down on his sleeping bag. He felt bad that he'd turned around.

Maybe Pete was right. Maybe he was a wimp.

Mark was tired, so he fell asleep for a little while.

He woke up when he heard his dad's voice. "How was your climb?"

"Great." Mark looked away and yawned.

"Where's Pete?" Dad asked.

Mark shrugged. "I don't know. Somewhere around."

Chapter 8

Lost in the Fog

Pete was starting to worry. It was very hard to see the trail in the mist, and he kept straying off it.

He came to a place where the trail branched into two trails. He didn't remember noticing it on the way up. He had no idea which way to go. If he chose the wrong trail he might end up in the waterfall. Maybe he'd been on the wrong trail all along.

Pete began to shiver.

He was lost.

He rubbed his hands together to warm them. His socks felt wet. He knew wet clothes were dangerous. He stamped his feet and wiggled his toes. They felt numb.

I'll probably die out here, he thought, and Mark will think it's his fault.

Then a sound made Pete jump. A moaning, coming from nearby.

It sounds like a trapped animal, Pete thought.

Then he remembered the strange ram's skull.

Chapter 9

It's All My Fault

Pete wasn't back for supper. Mark knew he had to tell the truth. He felt really bad.

Dad didn't yell at Mark or blame him. He called the park rangers and reported Pete missing.

Waiting was the worst part. Nobody felt like eating.

I shouldn't have let him go alone, thought Mark.

He imagined Pete's body bouncing from rock to rock like the water bottle.

His mom put an arm around him. "It will be okay," she told him. Mark didn't believe her. He knew she was scared too.

It was almost dark when a police car drove into the campsite. A policeman and two rangers climbed out. Pete wasn't with them.

"I'm really sorry," said the policeman. "It's almost impossible to see through the fog. We'll have to look again in the morning."

Pete might not make it through a night up there. It was so wet and cold.

Just then, a figure walked out of the thick fog.

It was Pete! Mark and his parents ran over to him.

"We thought you were dead," said Mark.

"I would have been," Pete replied, "if it hadn't been for this." He held up the ram's skull. "I know it sounds weird," Pete told his brother, "but when I was really lost, I heard that moaning sound and walked toward it. It led me back to the skull."

Mark looked at the skull. "Told you it was creepy," he whispered.

Pete put the skull on the ground. "It made a moaning sound when I was going the right way. If I went the wrong way it was quiet. That's how I made it back."

Mark smiled. "I'm glad you made it back okay," he said to his brother.

"Me too," said Pete. "Next time we go climbing, we should stay together."

Later, they climbed into their tent and zipped up the doorway.

A few feet away, the ram's skull gave off a white glow and a sound like laughter echoed from its mouth.

About the Author

Chris Buckton has been writing stories in her head all her life, but has only had the time to write them down since retiring from her job as a teacher and advisor. She has written three children's novels and about 25 short stories. She says, "What I love about writing is that I can travel anywhere I like, through time as well as space, and can invent characters to travel with. There's nothing more exciting." Chris and her husband live in a 500-year-old cottage near Cambridge, England, where she grew up.

About the Illustrator

Paul Savage works in a design studio, drawing pictures for advertising. He says illustrating books is "the best job." He's always been interested in illustrating books, and he loves reading. Paul also enjoys playing sports and running.

He lives in England with his wife and their daughter, Amelia.

Glossary

campsite (KAMP-site)—a place used for camping, where a tent is often set up

compass (KUHM-puhss)—an instrument for finding directions

energy (EN-ur-jee)—the strength to do active things without getting tired

Everest (EV-uh-rest)—Mount Everest is the world's highest mountain

forecast (FOR-kast)—the prediction for the weather

impossible (im-POSS-uh-buhl)—unable to be done

muffled (MUHF-uhld)—when a sound is made quieter, it is muffled

ram (RAM)—a male sheep. Rams have horns and often live in mountain areas.

ranger (RAYN-jur)—someone in charge of a park or forest

steep (STEEP)—sharply sloping

worthwhile (wurth-WYL)—useful and valuable

Discussion Questions

1. The brothers in this book had an argument. Who was right, Pete or Mark? Should they have kept climbing, or should they have gone down the mountain? Explain your answer.

2. Mark thinks it is his fault that Pete hasn't returned from the climb. Why does he think that? Have you ever felt guilty about something that happened to another person?

3. Can you explain how the ram's skull helped Pete find his way back down the mountain? If he hadn't found the skull, what else could he have done to save himself?

Writing Prompts

1. Mark and Pete make a list of things to take on their climbing trip up the mountain. You can read their list on page 7. Make your own list of things you would need to survive if you were going on a dangerous climbing trip.

2. At the end of this book, Pete returns. If he had not come back to the campsite, what would have happened next? Write a short story that explains what would have happened if Pete hadn't returned.

3. Have you ever gone camping or hiking? Write about your experience. Don't forget to describe what the area looked like! If you haven't gone camping, describe what you think it might be like.

IF YOU LIKED "SURVIVE"...

Killer Sharks
by Stan Cullimore

The Brown family is relaxing on their speedboat when, suddenly, deadly sharks surround them — but these are no ordinary sharks. Who sent the killer sharks? And will the Browns get out alive?

Code Breakers
by J. Powell

Brad, Conor, and Scott are bored — until they find the briefcase. When they discover a phone number inside, it leads them from clue to clue and eventually to a cold, damp cave. What is at the end of the trail?

... YOU'LL ALSO LIKE THESE BOOKS!

Sleepwalker
by J. Powell

When Josh decides to follow Tom one night on one of his sleepwalking adventures, real life suddenly turns into a nightmare!

Summer Trouble
by Jonny Zucker

Tom's summer plans change when his cousin decides to visit. He believes his entire vacation will be ruined . . . until Ben comes to his rescue in a rough situation.

INTERNET SITES

Do you want to know more about subjects related to this book? Or are you interested in learning about other topics? Then check out FactHound, a fun, easy way to find Internet sites.

Our investigative staff has already sniffed out great sites for you!

Here's how to use FactHound:

1. Visit *www.facthound.com*

2. Select your grade level.

3. To learn more about subjects related to this book, type in the book's ISBN number: **1598898523**.

4. Click the **Fetch It** button.

FactHound will fetch the best Internet sites for you!